P9-CSH-303

/
Ac57a

Araminta's Paint Box

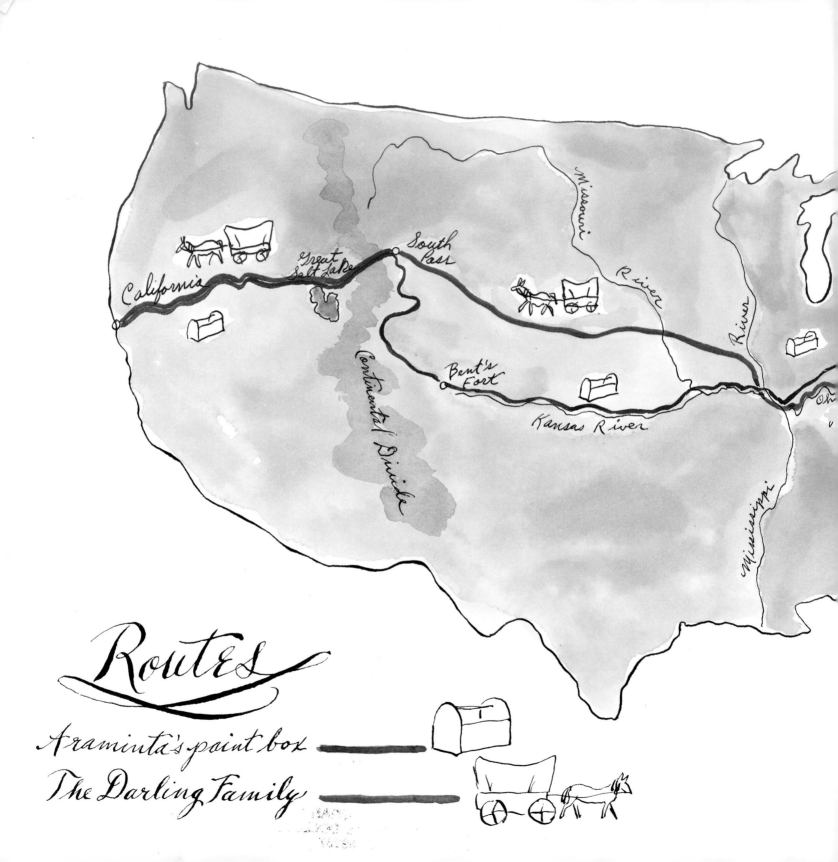

Araminta's Paint Box

by Karen Ackerman
illustrated by Betsy Lewin

ATHENEUM   1990   NEW YORK

RETA E. KING LIBRARY
CHADRON STATE COLLEGE
CHADRON, NE 69337

For Giuliette
—K. A.

*To Nunny Soderlund, Willard Dominick, Betty Harris,
and John Filsinger, with gratitude and good memories.*

B. L.

Text copyright © 1990 by Karen Ackerman
Illustrations copyright © 1990 by Betsy Lewin

All rights reserved.

Atheneum
Macmillan Publishing Company
866 Third Avenue, New York, NY 10022
Collier Macmillan Canada, Inc.
First Edition
Printed in Singapore

Library of Congress Cataloging-in-Publication Data
Ackerman, Karen.
Araminta's paint box / by Karen Ackerman;
illustrated by Betsy Lewin.—1st ed.   p.   cm.
Summary: When her family moves from Boston to California in 1847,
Araminta and her paint box become separated, but through a series of
new owners, the paint box finds its way to California.
ISBN 0-689-31462-0
[1. Overland journeys to the Pacific—Fiction.   2. Frontier and
pioneer life—Fiction.]   I. Lewin, Betsy, ill.   II. Title.
PZ7.A1824Ar   1990   [E]-dc19   88-35033   CIP   AC

E+
Ac57a

In 1847, Dr. Marcus Darling lived in the city of Boston,
Massachusetts, with his wife, Emilia, and his young daughter,
Araminta.

Dr. Darling was well respected in Boston. He worked long hours
and sometimes drove his buggy for miles to bring a baby into the
world, or set a broken leg, or tend a snakebite. He was a very good
doctor, and both Emilia and Araminta were proud of him.

Dr. Darling became so admired in Boston that he was offered a position as the very first doctor in a western town far away in a place called California. There was talk that California would soon become a state, which meant that settlers would begin moving west to buy land. Where there were people, there was need for a doctor.

The Darling family packed everything they could fit in a large wagon drawn by a team of strong draft horses. Emilia's beautiful old settee, the doctor's examining table, and Araminta's toy chest poked out of the back of the wagon, and cooking pots and pans clanged against the wagon sides where Emilia and Araminta had tied them.

Dr. Darling locked the front door of the family's lovely old Boston home, and with a slap of the reins, he and his family began their journey westward.

They followed the road to Scranton, Pennsylvania, where they planned to visit the doctor's only brother, who was a minister, and to rest themselves and the team of horses. The doctor and his brother hadn't seen each other for nearly ten years, so when he arrived, there was a lot of hugging and shaking hands and kissing cheeks.

Araminta's uncle, the Reverend Jacob Darling, had never even met her before. But before the doctor and his family left Scranton, Uncle Jacob gave Araminta a paint box to take with her to California.

"For my sweet niece on her journey," Uncle Jacob whispered to young Araminta, and he patted her cheek.

The Darlings waved good-bye, and Araminta held the paint box tightly in her arms as she sat in the back of the wagon.

Araminta's paint box was the most beautiful thing she had ever seen. It was nearly two feet long, and there were two rows of paint jars at the top. On each side of the handle, there was a deep hole filled with quills and brushes, and in the middle of the box was a thick roll of drawing paper wrapped in satin ribbon. Araminta touched every jar of paint and every quill and brush. She couldn't wait to begin a painting.

RETA E. KING LIBRARY
CHADRON STATE COLLEGE
CHADRON, NE 69337

They followed the road through Pennsylvania toward Ohio, where they would load their wagon onto a boat and ride the Ohio River to Illinois and then cross the great, muddy Mississippi.

The ride through the Pennsylvania farmlands was hot and dusty, and Araminta had a difficult time painting in the back of the wagon. The dust whirled up and stuck to the wet paint and coated the bristles of her paintbrushes. Now and then, the wagon pitched to one side, going over a rock or bump, and the tin cup full of water for rinsing brushes would tip over and soak Araminta's skirt and petticoat.

When the wagon unexpectedly struck a boulder that had tumbled from a hillside, everything inside went flying into the air. Emilia's lovely settee sailed out and landed upside down in the road. Araminta's paint jars rolled out every which way, and the doctor's examining table tumbled out onto the road and stood upright, as if waiting for the doctor's next patient.

The doctor walked through the fields toward a farmhouse to find someone to help him replace the wagon's now broken wheel. The farm was owned by a Mennonite family named Friedlander, and Mr. Friedlander was willing to help.

But while the wagon was hoisted up and the broken wheel replaced, Araminta's paint box slipped out of their wagon. Araminta didn't notice that it was missing until the family had traveled too far to go back for it.

Araminta's beautiful paint box was lost.

Daniel Friedlander was helping his father tie hay bales one afternoon when he tripped over some kind of box lying in the field. It was a very nice paint box, though there were only four small jars of paint left in it. Two quills and a brush were inside, and there were several sheets of rolled-up drawing paper.

When he showed the box to his papa, Mr. Friedlander knew it had fallen out of the wagon that had broken its wheel on the road near his farm the week before.

"They won't be back for it now," Mr. Friedlander said to his son. "They'd miss the boat down the Ohio River if they turned back."

The paint box remained with the Friedlanders.

And the box proved to be very useful. Mrs. Friedlander used the paint to trim her kitchen walls in brightly stenciled hearts and flowers and curlicues. She used up all of the blue paint and half of the red.

Daniel drew pictures of his prize heifer on the sheets of drawing paper.

Mr. Friedlander used the box to carry his carpentry tools.

RETA E. KING LIBRARY
CHADRON STATE COLLEGE

One day Mr. Friedlander went to a barn raising for a young couple who were to be married the next week. Farmers from all over the county came to help raise the new barn on the farm where the young couple would live after their wedding. Mr. Friedlander took his toolbox with him.

The groom's best man arrived in a coach from Illinois, and as soon as he stepped off the coach, he rolled up his shirtsleeves and set to work. Another passenger boarded the coach, bound for the Mississippi River.

But while the sides of the great barn were raised, the empty wooden box was mistakenly put on the coach by the driver. Before Mr. Friedlander noticed that the box had disappeared, the coach was rolling down the road back to Illinois.

Mr. Friedlander's toolbox was lost.

The coach driver stopped in Springfield to let off his passenger and have a hot bath and a good meal before going on farther north. The wooden box was taken from the coach and set near the passenger's steamer trunks.

The passenger was a riverboat gambler named Doolittle. He took another coach on to Hannibal, Missouri, where he boarded the riverboat *Blue Belle* on the Mississippi River. But he didn't notice the wooden box that was taken aboard the *Blue Belle* with his steamer trunks.

The box rode the great Mississippi southward.

Doolittle had a run of bad luck, and he lost his entire fortune in games of chance within a week. At the spot where the great Mississippi meets the Missouri River, he left the *Blue Belle*, and his steamer trunks and the wooden box were put on the dock. But, thinking the box belonged to someone else, Doolittle left it where it was.

The wooden box lay unclaimed on the dock for two weeks.

A young bride traveling west to meet her husband in Colorado waited at the same dock for a boat to carry her down the Missouri to the Kansas River and on to Bent's Fort. As she waited, she noticed a large wooden box lying nearby.

The young bride's husband, Captain Beaumont, was in Bent's Fort, training troops for battle in the war with Mexico. Expecting that the war would end quickly, he sent word for his wife to join him, but Captain Beaumont had no idea that his wife was going to have their first child.

Young Mrs. Beaumont thought the large box would make a lovely bassinet for her new baby. After she inquired and was told that no one had claimed it, she had the box loaded with the rest of her cases.

The wooden box went down the Missouri River.

After taking another boat from the Missouri down the Kansas River, young Mrs. Beaumont boarded a coach to take her the rest of the way to Bent's Fort, where her husband would be waiting for her.

RETA E. KING LIBRARY
CHADRON STATE COLLEGE
CHADRON, NE 69337

But Bent's Fort was a flurry of activity when she arrived. Soldiers scurried about, packing their horses to ride south to New Mexico, where a battle was going on. Captain Beaumont unloaded his wife's cases quickly, apologized to her for having to leave, and rode off through the high gate of Bent's Fort, with his cavalry troops thundering behind him.

Mrs. Beaumont managed to settle in by herself, but by the time she noticed that the wooden box was not with her cases it was too late. The captain had left the box on the coach, not realizing it belonged to his wife.

Mrs. Beaumont's baby bassinet was lost.

The coach traveled from Bent's Fort to the South Pass at the base of the Continental Divide. The only passengers were a Mormon family, who were let off at the edge of the South Pass. They planned to cross the mountain range on horseback and go westward to a new community on the Great Salt Lake settled by Mormons from the East.

The family was named Callagher, and Elijah was their youngest son. Elijah was the first to notice the large wooden box laid atop his family's baggage when the coach let them off at the edge of the pass.

"Whose is it, Papa?" he asked his father, who called out to the coach to come retrieve it, but the coach driver did not hear him.

The box crossed the mountains, tied to the saddle of Elijah's horse.

When the Callaghers arrived at the Great Salt Lake, the whole community came out to greet them. Each family had made the same journey and knew how difficult it was to leave everything behind in the East for a new life out West. First, the Callaghers were driven in a neighbor's wagon to see the Great Salt Lake, which was the center of the new settlement.

The other families arranged for a group supper to welcome the Callaghers. Tables were set up along the shores of the lake, and all of the Mormon families in the area attended the picnic. Each family offered a blessing at the table for the newcomers.

The other children gathered around Elijah to ask him where he'd come from and what school grade he was in.

Meanwhile, an old prospector drove his mule southeast along the Oregon Trail. The gold rush had just begun in California, and the prospector wanted to be among the first to stake a claim. He followed the trail to the edge of the Great Salt Lake, where it curved westward and joined the California Trail.

When he reached the junction of the two trails, the prospector saw a group of people gathered at the edge of the lake. They were having supper, and the prospector needed fresh water and food supplies.

He urged his mule down to the lake shore. When he asked for fresh water and a bit of jerky or beans, he was happily given a plate piled high with food. The prospector ate well and gave his tired mule a long rest.

The old prospector received much more than he had asked for. Several crates of supplies were tied to his mule's pack, and each family gave him something for his journey.

But the Callaghers had left nearly all of their belongings back East. So Elijah offered the prospector the wooden box.

The box would be just the right size to carry nuggets with California gold running through them, so the prospector accepted the box with thanks.

Tied to the end of the old prospector's mule pack, the box went to California.

The old prospector mined for months in the hills before he found gold. Then he loaded the wooden box with nuggets streaked with yellow gold and walked to town to file his claim at the land office.

But as the old prospector stepped through the thick weeds at the edge of the town, he felt a sharp pain in his ankle. He'd been bitten by a snake.

He hobbled to town as quickly as he could and fainted cold on the steps of the local doctor's office.

The doctor rushed out and carried him into his office, where he gave the old prospector some snakebite medicine and cleaned and dressed the wound.

When the old prospector woke, he told the doctor that he could pay him in gold for his help. The doctor's young daughter was sent outside to bring in the old prospector's mining box, which had been left on the steps where he had fainted.

Although the old prospector became very rich and famous because of his gold claim, the doctor who had saved his life did not want any more than the wooden mining box for payment.

Dr. Darling planned to make a paint box out of it, like the one his daughter, Araminta, had lost long before on their journey to California.